Just Say Hello

By: Rebecca Porter

To Stella
change begins
with you.

Printed in the United States of America

First printing 2020

ISBN 978-1-7353392-0-7 (paperback)

ISBN 978-1-7353392-1-4 (e-book)

For my amazing daughter Kiara,
whose unique differences
changed my world.

Deep in the hills lived a small community of elves. Every elf looked exactly the same, with straight silky brown hair, bright blue eyes, and long pointed ears. When an elf was born the sun shined brightly and the little elf cried.

Every day, the elves did the same things, day in and day out. The little elves would go to school, come home, and play ball while the adults worked, making sure not a leaf was out of place in their village.

One beautiful morning, two twin elves were born. The first was a little boy. He cried so loudly! His parents named him Kameron. The second born was a little girl. Instead of crying, she laughed and giggled.

Her parents were shocked!
"How can this be?" thought Mommy elf.
"Hello, little girl. "Your name will be
Kiara," she said, holding both baby elves
very tight.

Kiara's laugh was heard throughout the village.

As soon as the mayor heard the laugh, he quickly went to see where the noise was coming from.

The mayor walked in and asked, "What is that laughing?" with a puzzled look on his face. "Her hair is not straight it is curly. Her hair is not brown it is blonde. Her eyes are not blue they are green. Her ears are not long and pointy, they are small and round. And she is not crying, she is laughing. Kiara is different, and we are not. Just look at her and listen to that laugh!"

Mommy and Daddy elf stood up and said,
"She might be different. But she is just like you and me. Just look at her beautiful face, that little nose, her tiny fingers and toes, and her bright big smile."

The mayor only looked then walked away. He did not understand that Kiara was the same.

But Mommy and Daddy elf loved both baby elves, no matter what.

As the years went by, Kameron started to notice the different things Kiara would do.

"Why is Kiara different than me and my friends? Why doesn't she like school or play ball like the rest of us?"

Kameron sat next to his mom as he asked her.

"Well, Kameron," said Mommy elf,
"Just because Kiara doesn't look exactly like you, that doesn't mean you can't play with her.
She may not say much or play ball like you're used to, but she is still like you and me.
See, this is why she has you! You get to teach her everything you know. The more time you spend with her, the more things she will learn."

Kameron's eyes lit up, with the biggest smile on his face.

"**YES!**" yelled Kameron,

"That's exactly what I will do!"

Days, weeks, and months went by. Kameron only talked and spent all of his extra time with Kiara. He was so happy because she was no longer alone. He noticed that everything he taught her, she started to do.

One Afternoon Kiara, and Kameron were inside coloring.
Two little elves walked in and asked,
"Kameron, what are you doing? Kiara is different, just look at her hair. You're inside coloring when you should be outside playing ball with us."

Kameron stood up and said,
"Just because her hair isn't straight and brown, doesn't mean we can't play with her. Kiara may not say much or play ball like we are used to. But she is still like you and me. **SEE!** This is why I'm here; I get to teach her everything I know. All she needs is a friend to help her along the way. And most of all, she is opening my mind to newer adventures, which is a lot more fun."

The two little elves only looked then walked away. They did not understand that Kiara was the same.

High in a tree climbed the little elf. She was intrigued and wanted to read.

"Hello, Kiara. My name is Olivia. I really love your books, can I sit down and read some with you?"

Kiara looked at Halley with a smile on her face and simply said, "YES!"

They sat under the beautiful tree, reading book after book all day together.

That afternoon, three little elves
walked over to the tree and asked,

"Olivia, Kameron, what are you doing? Kiara is different. Just look at her eyes. You're outside reading books when you should be playing ball with us."

Olivia climbed down the tree and said, "Just because her eyes are not blue, doesn't mean we can't play with her. Kiara may not say much or play ball like we are used to, but she is still like you and me. **SEE!** This is why I'm here. I get to teach her everything I know. All she needs is a friend to help her along the way. And most of all, she is opening my mind to newer adventures, which is a lot more fun."

The three little elves only looked then walked away. They did not understand that Kiara was just the same.

One cold, snowy winter afternoon, a little elf walked up to Kiara wanting to play, "Hello, Kiara. My name is Daniel. I really love your snow fort and snowman. Can I play with you?"

Kiara looked up at him with a smile on her face and said, "Thank you, Daniel. **YES**, you can play."
That afternoon, they all played in the snow. They laughed and built snow forts and snowmen. Oh, it was so much fun.

Four elves walked towards Daniel and said,
"Daniel, what are you doing? Kiara is different. Just look at her ears. You're outside playing in the snow when you should be playing ball with us."

Daniel looked at them and said,
"Just because her ears aren't pointy doesn't mean we can't play with her. Kiara may not say much or play ball like we are used to, but she is still like you and me. **SEE!** This is why I am here. I get to teach her everything I know. All she needs is a friend to help her along the way. And most of all, she is opening my mind to newer adventures, which is a lot more fun."

This time was different. Instead of them walking away, all four elves picked up the snowballs and started to play.

"Hello, Kiara. My name is Laura"
"And my name is Kevin."
"Hi, my name is Anthony!"
"We really like your snowman, and this looks like so much fun.
Can we please play with you?"

Kiara looked at them with a smile on her face and picked up a snowball and started to say, "Hello Laura, Kevin, and Anthony. **YES.** You can play. But you have to catch me first!"

One **starry night** while every elf was laughing and playing in the snow, two elves were watching and talking from a distance.

"That looks like so much fun," said Michael sadly.

"Yes, it does." Agreed Jennet. "But we should be playing ball like we always do."

They both walked away. They did not understand that Kiara was just the same.

The very next day, Jennet and Michael walked up to Kiara with a sad look on their faces.

"Hello, Kiara. We really like your ball. It is not that much fun playing ball with just two elves." Michael said sadly. "Can we play ball with all of you?" asked Jennet.

Kiara looked at them with a smile on her face and said, "Of course, you can play ball with us. After all, it is my favorite thing to do.
It is just not fun playing ball all by yourself."

And on that day, all the little elves were outside playing, laughing, running around, but having fun most of all. This was the moment they all understood. Even though Kiara was different, she just needed a friend to help her along the way. But who learned the most were the little elves themselves. Every "hello" led them to new and exciting adventures.

All they had to do was walk up to Kiara and just say, "HELLO."

Why I wrote "Just Say Hello."

I wrote this book because my 11-year-old daughter, Kiara has down syndrome. I noticed how hard it was for her to make friends, and she would often play alone. I knew how much she could learn from other children if they only understood other children's differences. I want to make my book a teachable moment for other parents, and teachers. All it takes is a simple "Hello." And helping other kids understand that they can help those who don't yet know certain things. While learning something new themselves. I told my son the same thing I wrote in my book, "She has you to learn from, and if you take the time to teach her things that she does not know, Kiara will eventually learn." His smile, and reaction will be imprinted in my heart forever. And because he tells his friends the same thing I told him, they include her. My book teaches children to try and make friends with those that are different and understand that being different does not mean you cannot play with them. It just means they are unique in their own special ways. My story is also directed to children who have different hair, facial features, ethnicities, or cultures. I want children to know that if they open their minds to other's differences, it can lead them to new adventures. They might just make a friend along the way.

About the Author

Rebecca Porter is a mom of two beautiful children. Her daughter having Down Syndrome has encouraged her to start writing books about acceptance, and differences. She also illustrates all her books. "Just Say Hello," is the first of many books that she plans to publish.

Made in the USA
Monee, IL
14 August 2020